DATE DUE

P9-DDM-200

# Singing Down the Rain

*To the townsfolk of Cairo, Illinois,*
*who are big on hospitality and large of heart,*
*with thanks from a wandering writer*
*—J.C.*

*To Peg and Peter Scholtes,*
*for your love of children*
*—J.S.G.*

*I would like to thank my models Tiffany McKenzie*
*and Peter Kosman, as well as the other children who modeled,*
*and also Liz Rudenga and Sheryl Wiers of the*
*Trinity Christian College and the Young Authors Festival.*
*— Jan Spivey Gilchrist*



Library of Congress Cataloging-in-Publication Data
Cowley, Joy.
Singing down the rain / by Joy Cowley ; illustrated by Jan Spivey Gilchrist
p. cm.
Summary: In the midst of a severe drought, a mysterious woman drives into town claiming she specializes in rainsongs.
ISBN 0-06-027602-9.
[1. Droughts—Fiction. 2. Rain and rainfall—Fiction. 3. Singing—Fiction. 4. Afro-Americans—Fiction.]
I. Gilchrist, Jan Spivey, ill. II. Title
PZ7.C8375Sk 1997b 96-43055
[E]—dc20 CIP
AC

Typography by Alicia Mikles
1 2 3 4 5 6 7 8 9 10
❖
First Edition

# Singing Down the Rain

BY JOY COWLEY

ILLUSTRATED BY JAN SPIVEY GILCHRIST

HarperCollinsPublishers

My, but it was hot that afternoon!
When they got to Mr. Williams' store,
Brianna went under the oak
with Sharon and Tyrone
and the other children.
She set herself down on ground
that was baked bare as piecrust.

Her momma got a chair on the porch
with all the grown folks
and fanned herself with her hat.
"I never did see the likes
in all my born days," she sighed.
"We've got to get some rain soon,
or the corn will surely die."

SODA
POP
89¢
POTATOES
49¢ lb.
GRITS
99¢
LETTUCE

Mr. Williams rocked back and forth.
"Sweet wonder!" he groaned.
"River's no more than mud.
Air's so thick, you have to cut it up
to breathe it."

"Talking don't do a thing to make it better,"
snapped old Miss Bridges.

"Talking makes me feel better,"
said Mr. Williams sharply.
"You give me a two-day rain
and I'll gladly shut my mouth."

Brianna glanced at them.
The hot spell had gone on so long
that good and kind neighbors
were getting real scritchy with each other.
Even polite conversation was drying up.

She lay back and looked through brown leaves
at a blue jay that huddled with closed eyes
and drooping wings.
Beside her on a branch, a cricket sat
as still as a dead twig.

Tyrone bumped her arm and said,
"Someone's heading this way."

Sure enough, a cloud of yellow dust
was rolling down the road,
and in front was a blue pickup truck
speeding like it was going somewhere
important.

The truck didn't turn off down the highway.
It came into town and slowed to a stop
right outside Mr. Williams' store.
Out jumped a fine small woman
with bangles on her arms,
painted parrots in her ears,
and a smile so big,
it used most of her face.

Everyone sat up straight
to watch the way that woman walked
to the steps of the store.
"You folks need me?" she asked,
her parrots dancing 'round her ears.

Mr. Williams had stopped rocking.
"Well, no, ma'am. Can't say we do."

"You sure now?" she said.
"Because coming down that road,
I felt a praying and a needing.
I most certainly felt it in my bones."

Mr. Williams shook his head.
"The only thing we need here
is a mighty good shower of rain."

The woman laughed.
"Sir, that's what I'm referring to!
I happen to specialize in rainsongs."

POTATOES
49¢ lb.
LETTUCE
125¢

"Rainsongs!" Brianna whispered to Tyrone.

"Rainsongs!" he whispered back.

"What'd she say?" Miss Bridges asked.

"It's my profession," said the woman.
"You-all want a shower to come?
You have to ask for it real sweet.
Try singing it down, like this!"
She lifted her arms, jingling her bracelets
like a storm of silver bells.
Then she clapped and swayed,
singing in a high strong voice,

"*Oo-sha-la! Bo-ba-lo-lee!*
*Oo-sha-la! Bo-ba-lo!*
*Oo-sha-la! Bo-ba-lo-lee!*
*Oo-sha-la! Bo-ba-lo!*"

It seemed to Brianna
that the song rose as a cool wind
to fill all the spaces of sky,
but that was maybe her imagination.

The porch folks kind of smiled,
not knowing what else to do,
and went back to their talk
and their rocking.

*"Oo-sha-la! Bo-ba-lo-lee!*
*Oo-sha-la! Bo-ba-lo!"*

A haze like thin milk
spread across the sun.
It hung there for a few seconds,
then disappeared.

The woman stopped singing.
She stood in front of the porch steps,
her arms stretched wide.
"You folks got a mighty strong dryness here.
One voice is not enough. You-all want rain?
Sing! Come on now! Open up!
Sing out your wanting to the sky."

Brianna's mother held her hat over her face.
Mr. Williams looked sideways
with his eyebrows climbing up.
Miss Bridges plain laughed out loud,
and the others pretended to be busy.

The woman clapped her hands
and started up again.

*"Oo-sha-la! Bo-ba-lo-lee!*
*Oo-sha-la! Bo-ba-lo!"*

Brianna turned her head.
What was that echo?
A deep pulsing sound
was rising from the dried-up river.
Frogs! Hundreds of little green frogs
were feeling the rainsong cool on their skin
and were swelling out their throats.
*Brock! Brock! Brock!*

Then the cricket on the oak tree
jumped to another branch
and scraped its wings like fiddle bows.
*Zzz-it! Zzz-it! Zzz-it!*

The blue jay woke up,
put its head on one side,
and shook its feathers.
*Aw! Aw! Aw! Aw!*

A gray mist formed in the sky,
and wind rustled the dried leaves.

Still it was not enough.

"Sing! Sing!" begged the woman.

The folks on the porch
just slid their eyes 'round
and pretended she wasn't there.

Brianna could smell the rain
only a song or two away.
She got up and stepped over
to the rainsong woman.
She raised her hands in the air
and began with small sounds.

*"Oo-sha-la! Bo-ba-lo-lee!
Oo-sha-la! Bo-ba-lo!"*

Sharon came up behind her,
then Tyrone and the other children.
The woman smiled and waved them close
with her silvery jingling arms,
so close, they were touching each other.
They swayed in a bunch
like trees in the wind,
clapping their hands above their heads
and singing in clear strong voices.

*"Oo-sha-la! Bo-ba-lo-lee!*
*Oo-sha-la! Bo-ba-lo!"*

What a song there was now!
It was wide enough to fill the town,
the riverbed, and the fields of corn.
It reached up so high
that it hung mountains of cloud in the air
and started the rumbling of thunder.

It was too much for Brianna's mother.
She let go her hat and stepped right down
beside them, looking at the sky
and singing in her big church voice.

*"Oo-sha-la! Bo-ba-lo-lee!*
*Oo-sha-la! Bo-ba-lo!"*

Some drops of rain fell.
They splashed steaming on the steps.
They rolled like dusty beads on the road.

"Sweet wonder!" cried Mr. Williams.

Next thing, the clouds let go a waterfall.
Rain bounced on the bare earth
and turned to mud.
Rain made a drumbeat
on the roof of the store.
Rain poured into trickles and streams
that flowed down to the river.

Another moment and all those porch folk
were out of their rocking chairs
and down there with the children
and Brianna's mother,
stomping in the mud
and laughing fit to die.

None of them knew it
when the woman drove away.
Mr. Williams and Miss Bridges
were doing their own singing now,
dancing wet to the skin, faces up,
drinking all that mighty good rain,
like the frogs,
like the crickets,
like every other blessed creature
in that place.

One moment the pickup truck was there
and the next it was gone.
Only Brianna saw it,
hightailing off down the road.

Well, all that happened a little while ago.

Now, in that town,
the grass is green, the corn is yellow ripe,
and the river runs sweet down to the pool
where Brianna and Tyrone swim
and neighbors have their picnics.

But far away,
in a town where the sun is like fire
and the earth has dried to dust,
a blue pickup truck stops.
A fine small woman gets out,
and a song fills the air
like a cool breeze.

*"Oo-sha-la! Bo-ba-lo-lee!*
*Oo-sha-la! Bo-ba-lo!*
*Oo-sha-la! Bo-ba-lo-lee!*
*Oo-sha-la! Bo-ba-lo!"*

Sweet wonder!